Smiles for Grace

WRITTEN BY **BONNIE REBER** AND **STACEY ADAMS**
ILLUSTRATIONS BY **STACEY ADAMS**

Published by:
Books for All Foundation
13600 King Street, Apt 627
Overland Park, KS 66221

Published in the United States of America

ISBN: 978-0-9836236-1-8
Library of Congress Control Number: 2011909471

www.booksforallfoundation.org

This book is dedicated to all who helped bring this story to life. We would like to offer a special thanks to the team at Drumright Dental Center for supporting this project, sharing their expertise, and placing such importance on literacy and education.

Mama says, "Grace, we are going to see the dentist today. The dentist will look at your teeth."

I know about teeth.
I brush my teeth every day.

My friends at the office greet me.
"Hi, Grace. We are happy to see you."

I know what's next.
Yay! It's my turn to see the dentist.

The assistant says,
"Grace, please wait in this room."

I know this room.
I can see my cartoons
on the television.
I can see my teeth
on the screen.

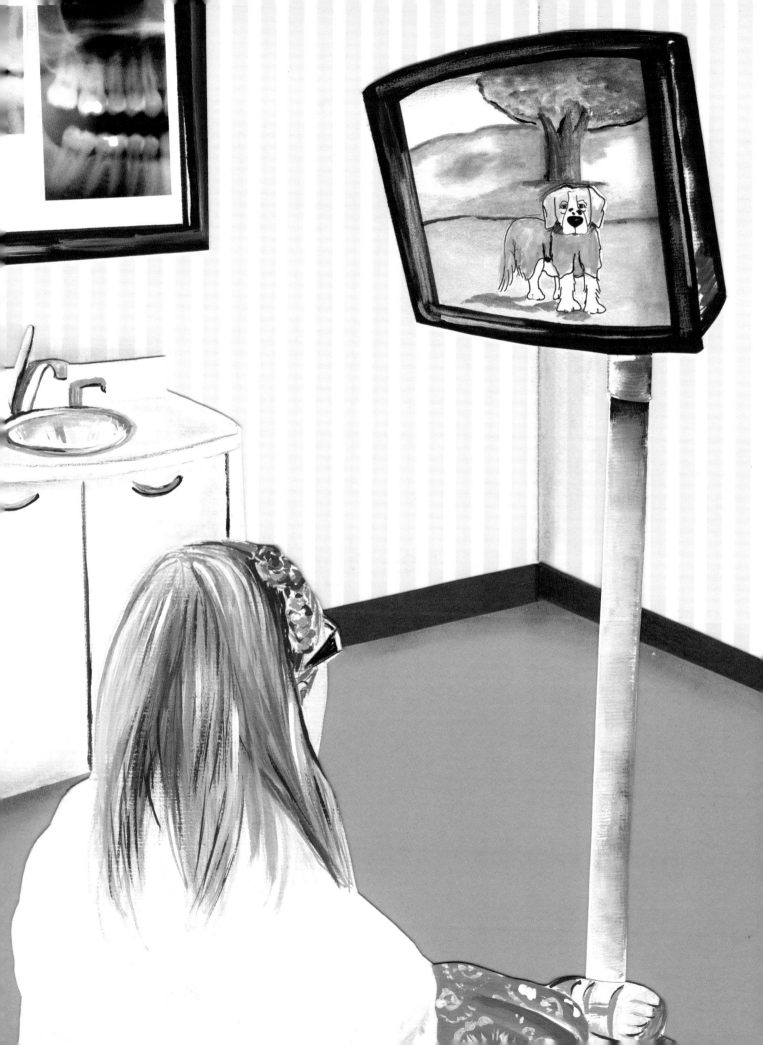

The dentist comes in.
"Hi, Grace, it's time to count your teeth. One, two, three..."

I know the dentist.
He wears gloves and a mask.

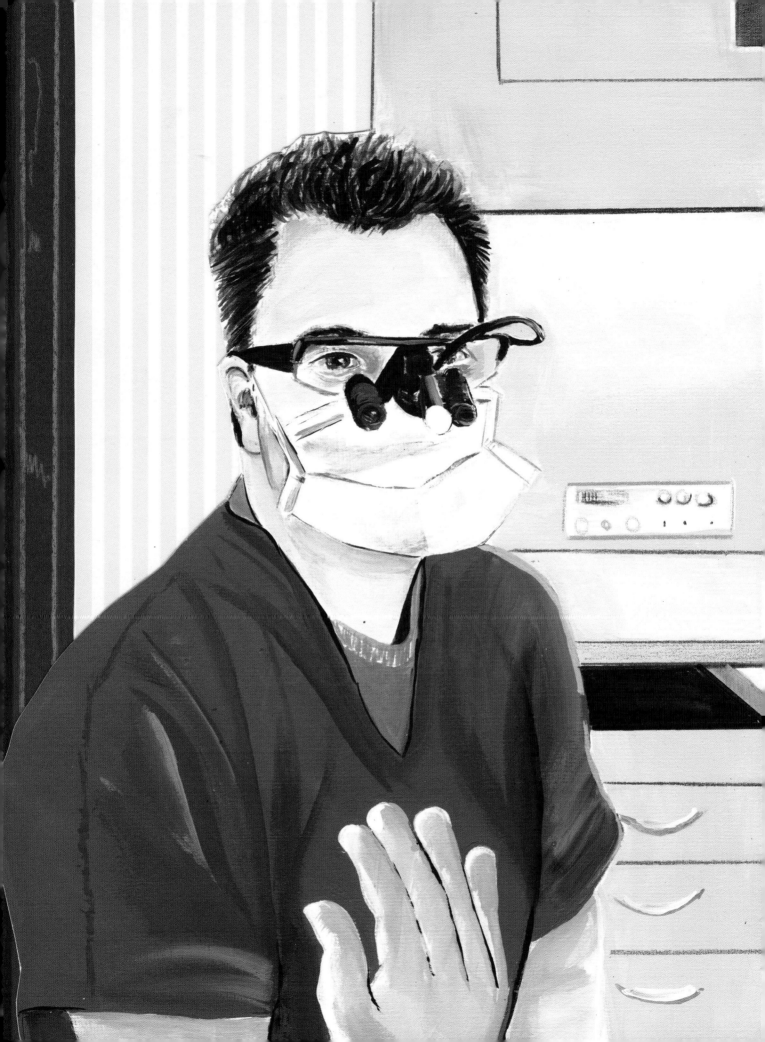

The dentist says,
"This may tickle a little bit."

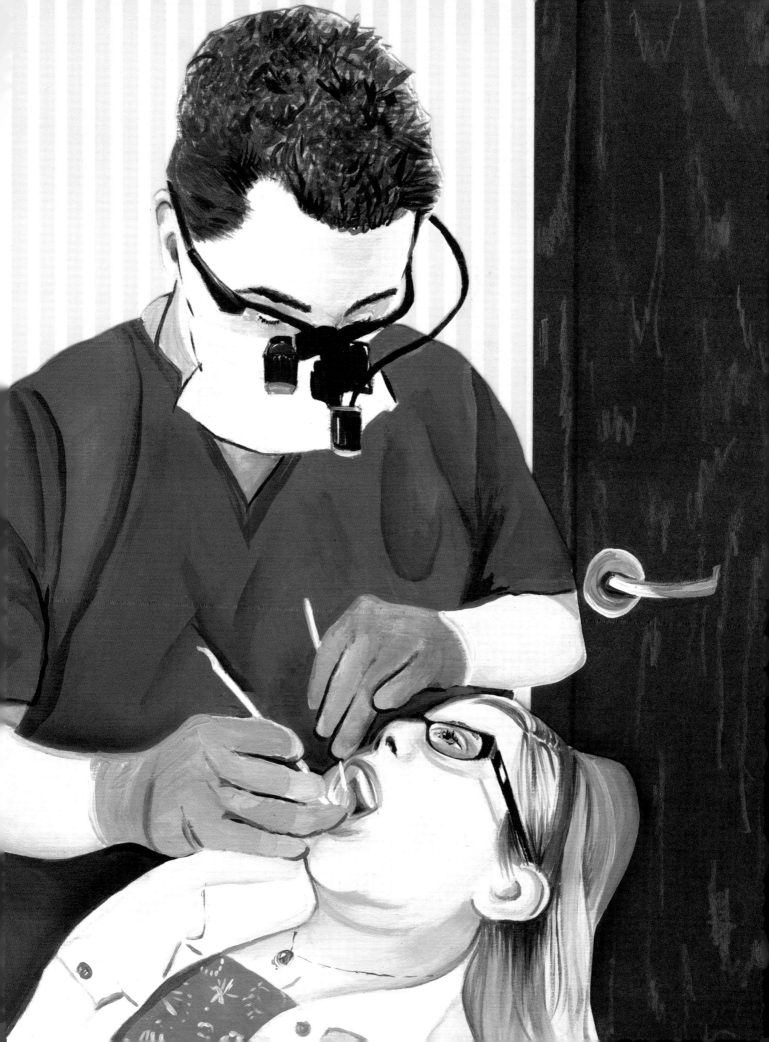

I know why.
I giggle when the water gun
washes my teeth.

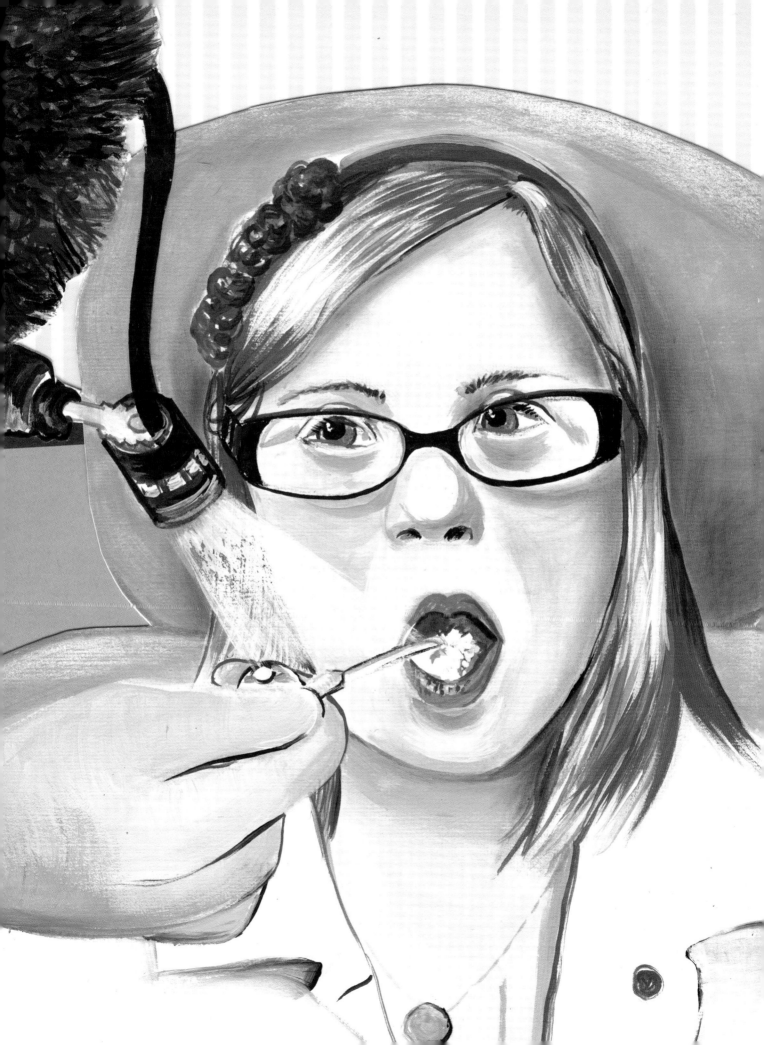

The dentist is finished.
"Grace, I'm so glad you came."

I know the dentist cares about me and wants me to be healthy.

The assistant says,
"Grace, you were so good.
You get a surprise!"

I can't wait to see my friends again!

AFTERWORD

Learn More: The Dentist

Teeth do lots of great things for you. They help you eat, help you speak, and give you a nice smile! Sometimes, we don't want to brush our teeth, but it is really important. Teeth, like the rest of our bodies, need to be taken care of daily as part of a healthy life.

A dentist is a type of doctor that focuses specifically on the teeth and mouth and helps us keep both clean and healthy. Dentists use special tools to clean and check the teeth. Some of these look funny or scary, but they are all very gentle, and the dentist will explain to you what
he is going to do with them. At the dentist, you will get your teeth cleaned, x-rayed to see how they are growing in, and fixed if there is anything wrong.

After going to the dentist, it is important to continue to take care of your teeth until your next visit. Brush your teeth every morning, after meals, and every night. Be sure to also floss at least once each day. This keeps plaque and bacteria from building up so you can keep smiling!

ABOUT THE AUTHORS

BONNIE REBER, a former elementary educator, is a strong advocate for inclusive opportunities for all children. Bonnie and her husband are the parents of 3 sons and daughter, Grace, with Down Syndrome.

STACEY ADAMS, a former educator of both art and special education, hopes to facilitate a love of independent reading while increasing literacy for students with both learning and physical challenges. Stacey and her husband have 3 daughters.

Smiles for Grace is the third in their series of accessible and inclusive children's books.